In memory of Nana and Pop
C F

To Ellie and Bethany with love
R T

This edition produced for
THE BOOK PEOPLE LTD
Hall Wood Avenue, Haydock,
St Helens WA11 9UL,
by LITTLE TIGER PRESS
An imprint of Magi Publications
1 The Coda Centre, 189 Munster Road,
London SW6 6AW
www.littletigerpress.com

First published in Great Britain 2003

ISBN 1 85430 843 2

Printed in Belgium by Proost

2 4 6 8 10 9 7 5 3

Goodnight, Sleep Tight!

Claire Freedman

illustrated by

Rory Tyger

TED SMART

One night, Grandma was looking after Archie.

"Aren't you sleepy yet, Archie?" asked Grandma.

"No!" replied Archie. "I don't feel sleepy at all. I'm wide awake!"

Grandma sat down on the edge of Archie's bed.

"Have you got all your favourite friends to cuddle up with?" she asked. "They might help you feel sleepy."

"I've got Tiger and Rabbit," said Archie. "But where's Elephant?"

"Here he is," said Grandma, tucking him in nice and snug. "You cuddle up and you'll soon feel sleepy."

But neither Archie nor his little friends went to sleep.

"We're still wide awake, Grandma," he said.

"What about a nice warm milky drink?" said Grandma. "That makes me sleepy."

Archie drank every
drop of his warm milk.
But he didn't feel sleepy.
"I'm still wide awake,
Grandma!" he said.
"Please can we watch
the fireflies? That might
make me sleepy."

Grandma wrapped Archie in his cosy blanket and together they watched the dancing fireflies. Archie tried to count them but it didn't make him feel sleepy.

"I'm still wide awake, Grandma!" he said. "Can you sing me a lullaby, please? That might make me sleepy."

Grandma sang some of
Archie's favourite songs.
Archie closed his eyes and listened . . .
but he didn't feel sleepy.

   "I'm still wide awake, Grandma,"
he whispered.

   "I know, Archie," Grandma said.
"Let me rock you in my arms. That
will make you sleepy."

Grandma rocked Archie gently in her arms, all the way down to the apple garden and back. Archie felt safe and warm in Grandma's arms, but he didn't feel the tiniest bit sleepy.

"Grandma, I'm STILL wide awake!" he said. "Will you tell me a story, please? Listening to stories makes me feel sleepy."

Grandma sat down comfortably, and
Archie snuggled up close to her.

She told him stories
about all the naughty
things his mummy
had done when
she was little
– just like him.

"Your mummy
never felt sleepy
at bedtime either,"
Grandma said.

Grandma carried Archie back inside.
She smiled a secret smile as she
remembered putting Archie's
mummy to bed when she
was little.

Grandma tucked Archie up in bed. She pulled the covers right up to his nose.

"I used to tuck your mummy up in bed, with the blankets pulled right up to her nose – like this!" said Grandma.

"Then I'd stroke the top of Mummy's forehead – like this," Grandma said.

Very gently she stroked the top of Archie's forehead.

"And I'd give Mummy a very special goodnight kiss," said Grandma.

Grandma gave Archie a special goodnight kiss.

"That's right, Grandma," said Archie
with a big yawn. "And then she says,
'Goodnight, sleep tight!'"
"That's right, Archie," said Grandma . . .

And before Grandma could even say "Goodnight, sleep tight", Archie was fast asleep!